R0083522565

09/2015

Cronus and the Threads of Dread

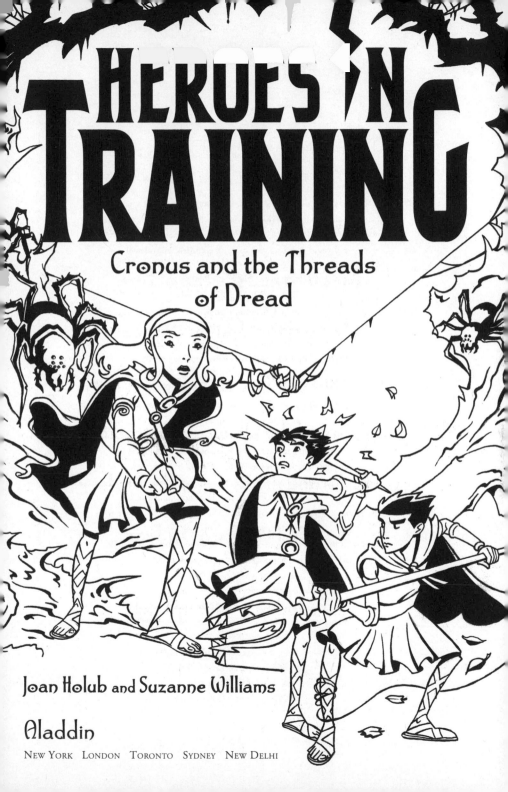

HEROES IN TRAINING

Cronus and the Threads of Dread

Joan Holub and Suzanne Williams

Aladdin

NEW YORK LONDON TORONTO SYDNEY NEW DELHI

ALADDIN

An imprint of Simon & Schuster Children's Publishing Division
1230 Avenue of the Americas, New York, NY 10020
First Aladdin hardcover edition December 2014
Text copyright © 2014 by Joan Holub and Suzanne Williams
Illustrations copyright © 2014 by Craig Phillips
Also available in an Aladdin paperback edition.
All rights reserved, including the right of reproduction
in whole or in part in any form.
ALADDIN is a trademark of Simon & Schuster, Inc.,
and related logo is a registered trademark of Simon & Schuster, Inc.
For information about special discounts for bulk purchases,
please contact Simon & Schuster Special Sales
at 1-866-506-1949 or business@simonandschuster.com.
The Simon & Schuster Speakers Bureau can bring authors to your live event.
For more information or to book an event,
contact the Simon & Schuster Speakers Bureau at 1-866-248-3049
or visit our website at www.simonspeakers.com.
Jacket designed by Karin Paprocki
Interior designed by Mike Rosamilia
The text of this book was set in Adobe Garamond Pro.
Manufactured in the United States of America 1014 FFG
2 4 6 8 10 9 7 5 3 1
Library of Congress Control Number 2014943703
ISBN 978-1-4424-8852-6 (hc)
ISBN 978-1-4424-8851-9 (pbk)
ISBN 978-1-4424-8853-3 (eBook)

For our heroic readers:
Kaitlin S., Eden O., Sven S., Jakob W., Billy F.,
Lana W., Tiffany W., John K., Kira W., Diamond C.,
Ariel S., Christine D-H. and Kenzo S., Nikolas M.,
Robby B., Kameron K., Trey H., Tyler E., Kyle Z.,
Vivian Z., the Andrade family, Gavin F., Caitlin R.,
and you!
—J. H. and S. W.

⚡ Contents ⚡

Greetings,
Mortal Readers,

I am Pythia, the Oracle of Delphi, in Greece. I have the power to see the future. Hear my prophecy:

Ahead I see dancers lurking. Wait—make that *danger* lurking. (The future can be blurry, especially when my eyeglasses are foggy.)

Anyhoo, beware! Titan giants seek to rule all of Earth's domains—oceans, mountains, forests, and the depths of the Underwear. Oops—make that *Underworld*. Led by King Cronus, they are out to destroy us all!

Yet I foresee hope. A band of rightful rulers called Olympians will arise. Though their size and youth are no match for the Titans, they will be giant in heart, mind, and spirit. They now follow their leader—a very special boy. One who is destined to become king of the gods and ruler of the heavens.

If he is brave enough.

And if he and his friends work together as one. And if they can learn to use their new amazing flowers—um, amazing *powers*—in time to save the world!

CHAPTER ONE

Sticky Spidernets!

Surrender, Olympians!

Nine young Olympians—Zeus, Hera, Poseidon, Hades, Hestia, Demeter, Apollo, Ares, and Athena—stared at the sky in horror. The words appeared in a huge spiderweb that had been spun between the clouds. The web looked like it covered the entire sky!

Suddenly, sticky strands shot down from the

clouds. One of them wrapped around Poseidon's ankle and yanked him away.

"Sticky spidernets!" he yelled.

Zeus, their leader, grabbed the lightning bolt attached to his belt.

"Bolt, large!" he commanded.

The magical weapon grew until it was as big as Zeus. Weeks before, he had pulled it from a stone in the Temple of Delphi. It had helped him battle all kinds of monsters, beasts, and the Crony army ever since.

Zeus ran after Poseidon as another thread shot down and grabbed Hestia's ankle. Then another thread grabbed Demeter around her waist, and the next one circled Hera's arm!

"Help!" they cried as the sticky threads dragged them away.

"What's happening?" Hades asked, catching up to Zeus as they chased after the four captured

Olympians. Apollo, Ares, and Athena followed at their heels.

"I don't know!" Zeus replied. "But I'm not going to lose any more Olympians—not again!"

As they got closer to the web, they could see a small army of spiders high above them, busy at work. Their round, black bodies were the size of melons. Their hairy legs were twice as long as the Olympians were tall.

"Spiders!" Apollo yelled.

"I'll take care of them!" cried Ares, the god of war. His red eyes flashed with anger. He raised the spear he carried and charged past Zeus.

"Taste the Spear of Fear!" he yelled, hurling the spear at the web strands. The spear was his own magical object, given to him by a bunch of Amazon warrior girls. The only problem? The spear was not a spear of fear—it was a scaredy-cat spear!

Whoosh! The spear whizzed toward one of the spiders. The creature swiftly moved out of the way. The spear cut through the sticky strands and got stuck in a tree.

A small spiderweb rolled down from the larger one. Words woven in it read:

Ha-ha! You missed!

"Not funny!" Ares fumed, and he stomped off to get his spear.

At the same time a thick strand of web reached down to grab Hades. He quickly dodged it. Then he put on his Helm of Darkness. He had found his magical object in the Underworld—the land of the dead, which he ruled. The helmet instantly turned Hades invisible.

"Can't catch me if you can't see me!" he taunted.

"But they can still hear you," Zeus pointed

out as three spiders skittered toward the place where Hades's voice had come from.

Ares pulled his spear out of the tree. "I won't miss again!" he promised, shaking a fist at the spiders.

Whack! He slashed at the nearest strand of web. The spear sliced clean through.

"We have to free Hera, Poseidon, Hestia, and Demeter!" Zeus cried. But the strands were pulling the four captured Olympians higher and higher off the ground. They had to act fast.

"Aaaaaaaaaaaaah!" With a battle cry Zeus jumped up and slashed at the strand holding Poseidon. Bolt sliced right through, and Poseidon fell to the ground with a thump. Apollo raced over and started to pull the sticky strands from him.

Whack! Ares cut through some strands with

his spear to free Hera. She thudded to the ground just like Poseidon. Athena ran to her aid.

Overhead the spiders began to furiously spin more webs. Zeus lunged at the strand holding Demeter, but the web yanked her out of reach. Then a strand came down to grab Zeus, brushing his leg. He jumped out of the way just in time.

"They're everywhere!" Ares yelled, hacking at the strands as they came down to grab him too.

Ares looks like he has things under control, though, thought Zeus. So he got busy slicing sticky webs between him and Hera and Poseidon. Up ahead he could see Athena rolling Hera out of the way as two strands tried to grab them both.

Poseidon and Apollo ran up to Zeus, breathless.

"We need to take shelter in the woods, bro!" Poseidon urged.

"But Hestia and Demeter . . . ," Zeus said.

"They're up in the clouds, I fear," said Apollo. "There is no way for us to get near." He often spoke in rhyme. And he carried a lyre since he was a musician.

Zeus looked up to see Hestia and Demeter being carried higher and higher, up toward the center of the web. Then he felt Poseidon yank his arm.

"Watch out!" Poseidon cried, pulling Zeus toward him.

A strand swung right past Zeus. Poseidon had saved him.

Zeus sighed. "You're right. We've got to retreat," he said reluctantly.

Zeus followed Poseidon and Apollo away from the web, to the safety of nearby trees. Athena and Hera had already taken shelter there. Hera was picking sticky pieces of web from her long, blond hair.

"Where is Ares?" Zeus asked, looking around. "And Hades?"

"Hades turned invisible, remember?" Apollo reminded him.

Zeus cupped his hands around his mouth. "Hades! Hades! Are you here?"

There was no answer.

Athena saw something shining in the grass a short distance away. She ran and grabbed it.

"Here's that shield Ares wore," she said, holding it up. The shield was made of tarnished metal. Gold tassels hung from it. "But no Ares."

Zeus's dark eyes flashed with anger and frustration.

"Rolling thunder!" he cried. "We keep losing Olympians!"

CHAPTER TWO

Goddess of What?

Zeus sank down to sit against a tree.

"What kind of leader keeps losing everybody?" he said. "Sometimes I don't understand why Pythia said that I'm the leader of the Olympians."

"Well, I've *never* understood it either," said Hera.

"Ha-ha," said Zeus flatly, kicking at the dirt with his boot.

His life had changed overnight. It had started when a bunch of Cronies had captured him. The half-giant soldiers of evil King Cronus had given him to the king himself as a delicious snack!

Zeus had escaped—along with Hera and Poseidon, who had been trapped inside Cronus's belly. They had met Pythia, the Oracle of Delphi. She'd told them they were Olympians. It was their destiny to overthrow King Cronus. But first they had to go on a bunch of quests and find more Olympians.

And that was what they'd been doing ever since. They'd fought monsters and giant half gods called Titans. They'd found out that Zeus, Hera, Hades, Poseidon, Demeter, and Hestia all had the same mom. Now they should have been nine Olympians strong—except that four were lost.

"I think you're a good leader," Apollo told Zeus. "You got us this far."

"Well, I just met you," Athena said to Zeus, "so I don't know if you're a good leader yet."

Before coming among the spiders, the Olympians had been trapped in a giant urn carried by the Cronies. Luckily, Rhea, the mother of Zeus and his brothers and sisters, had freed them. When the urn had broken, they'd realized that brown-haired, gray-eyed Athena had been inside with them the whole time.

Now, Athena held out the aegis to Zeus.

"Keep it," he said. "Pythia said it was yours, too. You should wear it."

"She also said that Athena was the goddess of cleverness," said Hera. "Why would such a goddess need a shield?"

Zeus knew that Hera was jealous. She had

waited a long time to find her own magical object. Then after she'd found it—a peacock feather that could spy on things and report back—she'd lost it.

Athena slipped the aegis over her head. "No idea why I'd need it. But it's kind of cool, so I might as well wear it," she said. Then she looked at Zeus. "So, what now?"

"Pythia said we had to find the center of a 'trouble spot' and find the Threads of Dread," said Poseidon. "So I guess we need to get to the center of that web?"

Zeus looked up at the sky. The huge web was stretched between the clouds. Getting to the center might take days—days with his friends still in danger!

He jumped up. "We need to find a path to the center that will let us avoid all those sticky strands," he said. "Hera, see if Chip can help us."

Hera grabbed the oval stone amulet she wore around her neck. Chip was a magical object too. It belonged to Zeus, but he didn't mind sharing Chip with Hera.

"Can you find us a path around the sticky spiderwebs, Chip?" Hera asked.

"I-ip an-cip ry-tip!" the stone answered her.

Athena's eyes got wide. "It talks! But what is it saying?"

"Chip speaks in a special language," Hera explained. "It's easy. You move the first letter of the word to the end of the word. Then you add 'ip.' Ee-sip?"

Athena frowned. "Um . . . sippy cup? Is that what you're saying?"

Hera rolled her eyes. "No, I said 'see.' And Chip said, 'I can try.' 'I-ip an-cip ry-tip.' Get it?"

Athena shrugged. "Um, sort of . . . not really."

"I thought she was supposed to be the goddess

of cleverness," Poseidon whispered in Zeus's ear.

"Well, she *was* stuck in that urn for a while," Zeus whispered back. "Maybe she's just warming up."

Hera started marching through the trees. "We should get as far as we can before dark," she said. "Come on!"

The four other Olympians followed Hera as they made their way to the center of the web. Zeus kept looking up at the giant words "Surrender, Olympians" woven across the sky.

"Something must be controlling those spiders," he said. "Spiders aren't smart enough to send us a message on their own."

"What message?" Athena asked.

Zeus pointed to the sky. "Uh, that big one there? The one that says 'Surrender, Olympians'?"

Athena squinted. "Oh, is that what it says? I thought it said 'Sugary Octopus.'"

"Seriously?" Poseidon asked, nudging Zeus.

Athena shrugged. "Yeah, I guess."

Apollo walked up next to her and strummed on his lyre. *"Athena, goddess, you are so new. Please tell us all something about you,"* he sang.

Athena smiled. "Well, I love to weave. I'm a great weaver," she said. "And I like to invent things."

"Like sugary octopuses?" Poseidon asked.

"Ha! That's pretty funny," Athena said cheerfully, and they kept walking.

As the sun set, Chip led them to a cave in the side of a hill.

"Nice job, Chip," Hera said, looking around. "Although I wish there were a stream nearby. I'm so thirsty."

"No problem," Poseidon said. He held up his magical object—a three-pronged trident. He struck it into the ground outside the cave, and clear water bubbled up from the earth.

"Hooray!" Hera said, and the five Olympians greedily drank the water.

"Now we just need some food," Poseidon remarked. "There's not much left in my pack except some crumbs of bread and cheese."

"I picked some wild grapes as we walked," Apollo said.

"Hey, my aegis is supposed to be magical, right?" Athena asked. "I'm going to try something."

She took off the aegis and placed it on the ground. "Okay, aegis, help me invent something new and delicious to eat!" she said.

Nobody expected anything to happen. But they all gasped when a small tree burst from the ground outside the cave. Small, oval, black fruit grew from the tree's gnarled branches.

"Those ovals look like shrunken plums,"

Poseidon remarked, picking one. "Let's see how they taste."

He picked one and bit into it. "Ow! My tooth!"

He spit out the tiny fruit. "This tastes terrible. And I think the pit inside it broke my tooth!"

"Well, they're my invention, so there must be something awesome about them," said Athena. She looked at the tree. "I shall call you 'owl love' because I love owls."

She picked up a stick and spelled out the word by scratching in the dirt.

"*O-L-I-V-E*," Hera read the letters out loud. "That's not how you spell 'owl love.'"

"Well, that's how *I* spell it," Athena said.

"So I guess that makes this an olive tree," said Hera.

"Yuck. Olives are the pits!" Poseidon complained.

Athena picked up one of the olives. "Who else wants to try one?"

The other Olympians looked down at the ground.

"Um, no thanks," Zeus said.

Athena popped one into her mouth. She started to make a face, then forced a smile.

"It's, um, good," she said. But Zeus could tell she was hiding the olive in her cheek.

Poseidon leaned over to Zeus. "What is up with this girl?" he whispered.

CHAPTER THREE

Stuck on Each Other

ell, I'm sorry you guys didn't like my new food invention," Athena said.

The five Olympians were sitting around a campfire outside the cave. They ate a small meal of the wild grapes Apollo had picked, plus whatever food was left in their packs.

"It's not so bad," Poseidon said. "The branches make good firewood."

Athena's gray eyes narrowed, like she wasn't

sure if he was teasing her or not. "I bet I'm great at inventing musical instruments too. I'll show you."

She stood up and started walking around the camp. A few moments later she came back with a hollow reed and a sharp stick.

"I just need to poke some holes in this reed," she said. She got to work, her tongue sticking out in concentration.

Zeus and Poseidon looked at each other. What was she up to now?

Then she held up the reed. "Done!" she said proudly.

"So, what is it?" Hera asked.

"I'm . . . I'm not sure," Athena admitted. "I think you blow into it."

She held the reed in one hand and covered one of the ends with her other hand. Then she started to blow into the little holes. Her face turned bright red with effort, but no music came out.

"Nice try, I guess," said Poseidon.

Athena put down the reed. Her face was still red, but Zeus was pretty sure it was because she was embarrassed.

"I'm going to sleep," she said.

Zeus nodded. "Good idea for all of us. I want to leave as soon as the sun's up. The others are out there somewhere, waiting for us to rescue them."

They all headed into the cave to sleep.

Zeus woke up as soon as the first rays of morning sunlight brightened the cave. He stood up, stretched, and walked outside. Right outside the cave something stopped him in his tracks— something that felt very familiar. A web! He knocked it away fast. What in Bolt's name was going on?

There were spiderwebs everywhere now! They stretched between trees and rocks and bushes as far as he could see. He looked up at the sky and saw a new message in the web. It read: *You can't escape!*

"Hey, guys, you need to see this!" Zeus called out.

The others came out of the cave, sleepily rubbing their eyes.

"No way!" Poseidon cried, staring.

Hera gasped. "They're everywhere."

Athena turned pale. "Are there lots of spiders out there too?"

Zeus looked around. "I don't see any," he said. He took Bolt from his belt. "Bolt, large!"

Bolt expanded, and Zeus hacked at the nearest spiderweb, cutting right through it.

"Poseidon, try your trident," he said.

"Sure," Poseidon said. He started slashing at

the webs with it. The trident didn't cut as cleanly as Bolt, but it chopped through them okay.

Zeus turned to the other Olympians. "All right. Here's the plan. Hera, ask Chip to take us to the heart of the web, and fast! Poseidon and I will walk in the front. We'll cut through the webs, and the rest of you can follow."

"Right. I'll get Chip on it," Hera said with a nod.

Poseidon created another bubbling fountain, and they all quickly drank and cleaned up. Then they made their way through the trees as Chip gave directions.

"O-gip ight-rip!" the stone amulet instructed.

"What's it saying?" Athena asked. "Abandon ship?"

"It's telling us to go right," Hera replied, shaking her head.

Athena studied the webs carefully as they

passed. "I think I know that pattern," she said, stopping to look at one web. "It's called a basket weave. Or maybe it's a satin weave. Or is it a twill?" She frowned, confused.

"Who cares what it's called? These webs are a sticky pain!" Poseidon complained. He pushed aside a web that Zeus had just cut. Then he tried to move forward, but stopped. "Hey, I'm stuck!"

Hera started peeling web off him. "Hold still."

Zeus sighed. "This is taking forever. We'll never catch up with those Olympian-snatchers."

"Maybe we need a song to cheer us up," Apollo said. "I just wrote one."

He began to strum his lyre and sing.

"I'm stuck on you.
You're stuck on me.

If we stick together,

How happy we'll be . . ."

"Can you please sing about something else besides being sticky?" Poseidon complained, brushing off more web strands.

Before Apollo could respond, a loud cry interrupted them.

"Heeeeeeeeeeelp!"

The Olympians looked at one another, surprised.

"It's coming from up ahead!" Zeus said, frantically hacking at the webs.

Moving on, he saw a young girl he'd never met before trapped in the webs. Her eyes lit up when she saw Zeus.

"Please! Can you help me?" she asked him.

"Stand still," Zeus said, starting to slice away at the web strands around the girl. The others caught up and pulled the strands away, setting the girl free.

"Thank you," said the girl. She wiped at her face and neck to get the last pieces of the webs off. "I was milking the goats this morning near our farm when the webs came down. I saw a really big spider and got scared and ran. But I got caught anyway."

"This stuff is easy to get caught in," Poseidon assured her.

"How far away is your farm?" Hera asked.

The girl pointed. "Just through those trees."

"We'll get you home," Apollo said. "And if you have any food to spare, we'd be happy if you could share."

The girl smiled. "Of course!"

They made their way to the farm. The trees opened up to a small field. Luckily, there were fewer webs here. The girl's parents rushed out to greet her.

"Alexia! You're safe!" her mother exclaimed.

"They saved me," the girl said with a nod toward the Olympians. "Can we get them some food?"

The grateful farmers filled the Olympians' packs with bread, potatoes, chunks of cheese, and bright red apples. When the farmers learned that the Olympians were headed to the center of the spiderweb, they were surprised.

"You all must be very brave if you're going to face whatever beast is spinning that web," Alexia's mother said.

"No, we just really, really love spiders," Poseidon joked.

Everyone laughed. Zeus said nothing. He wasn't feeling really brave right now. Those spidery messages were getting to him.

"Chip says to keep going east," Hera reported as they left the farm.

Zeus pointed. "So I guess we take that road over there."

The Olympians said good-bye to Alexia and her parents, then started off following Chip's directions.

The dirt road was well worn by wagon wheels. Web strands crisscrossed the path, their ends attached to trees and bushes on either side. Zeus found he could avoid webs by ducking.

"Keep low," he urged the others.

They obeyed, ducking to avoid the webs too. Zeus stared down at the road. Sunlight streamed through the webs above, casting a pattern of shadows.

Soon he found his mind wandering. He saw shapes in the shadows. *There's a tall man with long legs. That one looks like a snowy mountain. And that one up ahead looks like a giant spider—*

Zeus froze. He looked up. Uh-oh! High in the

branches of a tree sat a huge black spider. Zeus could see its beady red eyes and sharp fangs.

Behind him the other Olympians bumped into one another as they came to a sudden stop.

"Bro, what's the deal?" Poseidon asked.

"Sssssshhh!" Zeus warned, pointing upward. "Something tells me we're about to become spider food!"

CHAPTER FOUR

Nowhere to Hide

S pider food?" Athena whispered. She sounded terrified.

"Sssshhh," Zeus warned again. "It doesn't seem to see us. I think we can pass under it if we go quietly."

"And *don't* touch any part of the web," Hera added.

Zeus nodded and then slowly, carefully moved forward. Every once in a while he checked behind him. The other Olympians were moving slowly and quietly too. Athena was shaking with fear.

Zeus looked up. The spider sat there, still as a statue. But he didn't feel safe until the road finally veered right and the spider was far behind them.

"That was close," he said.

"Yeah," agreed Poseidon. "I'm glad we didn't get turned into spider meat."

Athena shuddered. "Please don't say that."

"Well, that spider might have been napping, but its friends have been busy," Hera said, pointing up. "Look!"

Another new message stretched across the sky.

The Cronies will find you!

"The ponies are fine? What does that mean?" Athena asked.

Hera rolled her eyes. "It says, 'The Cronies will find you.' And that means that King Cronus has his army out looking for us."

"Hey! I bet he's behind whatever is spinning those messages," Zeus added.

"Wait, you mean all those spiders in the sky aren't spinning the messages?" Poseidon asked.

"Those letters are *enormous*," Zeus pointed out. "Something bigger than spiders has to be helping make them. Besides, I'm not so sure spiders can even spell on their own. I've been thinking. Maybe there's something humongous waiting for us at the center of the web. Like another Creature of Chaos."

"What's a Creature of Chaos?" Athena asked nervously.

"A gross, nasty, mean, giant beast!" Poseidon replied. "We've battled all kinds of them. A giant python. Bees as big as horses. Birds made of metal. Weird warrior guys who hopped around on one foot. . . ."

"And you defeated them all?" Athena asked.

"Of course we did," boasted Hera. "King Cronus keeps sending them to stop us, but he hasn't succeeded yet!"

Athena looked thoughtful. "But why is King Cronus worried about a bunch of kids?"

"We're not kids. We're *Olympians*," Hera said pointedly. "Heroes."

"Heroes in training," Apollo reminded her.

Hera shrugged. "Whatever. We've been training pretty hard. And Pythia says we're supposed to overthrow King Cronus one day."

Something was stirring inside Zeus's brain. "You know, Athena asked a pretty good question. I mean, we *are* a bunch of kids. Yeah, we have some magical weapons, but King Cronus and his army are much more powerful. So there must be a reason he's so determined to stop us. Something he knows that we don't."

"Like what?" Poseidon asked.

"Like, maybe he knows for absolutely sure that we will defeat him," Zeus said. "Maybe he keeps trying to stop us because he's scared."

"Uh, and maybe not," Poseidon said. He tapped Zeus's shoulder and pointed to a nearby web with the words: *YOU should be scared.*

Zeus gulped.

"I didn't think that spiders had ears, but someone is listening to us, I fear," Apollo said.

"So, what now?" Hera asked. "The Cronies are looking for us, and the spiders are spying on us."

Zeus motioned for everyone to come closer. They formed a huddle.

"We have to keep heading for the center of the web," he whispered. "If we see any Cronies along the way, we'll deal with them then."

The other Olympians nodded. They broke out of the huddle to see another message in a web hanging from the nearest tree: *Nowhere to hide.*

"Just ignore it," Zeus sighed. "Let's go."

They kept walking. The tunnel they'd been traveling through in the webs ended, and they found themselves back on a path with webs crisscrossing in front of them. Zeus started hacking away with Bolt again.

"Look!" Hera called out. "The big message in the sky is changing."

They all looked up as a new message appeared for the world to read, stretching across the entire sky: *Mortals, save yourselves! Bring us the Olympians!*

"Oh, great," moaned Poseidon. "Not only do we have the Cronies after us, but now everybody else will be after us too!"

"Thankfully, no one's around," Zeus said.

"Oh, really?" asked Hera.

She pointed ahead. Swirls of chimney smoke could be seen over the next hill.

"Illage-vip traight-sip head-aip," Chip said.

"Did he say, 'Spit out your porridge'?" asked Athena.

Hera sighed. "He said there's a village straight ahead."

"So we'll go around it. We'll go off the road," Zeus said.

Poseidon frowned. "It's awfully webby there."

"It's the only way," Zeus said.

Then they heard the sound of footsteps and the roar of voices coming over the hill.

"Too late!" cried Hera. "The villagers are coming!"

"Quick! Into the trees!" Zeus commanded.

They ran off the path—and immediately got stuck in a tangle of webs.

"They're everywhere!" Poseidon wailed.

Zeus brushed a web away from his mouth. Some web strands had wrapped themselves around his legs, and he started hacking at them with Bolt. "I'll free myself and then help you guys," he yelled to the others.

"Hurry!" urged Hera, because her legs were trapped in web strands too.

Zeus cut away the webs holding him. The others were still hopelessly tangled. The sound of the villagers was getting closer and closer. Quickly, he freed Hera.

"Hey there! Are you all right?" called a voice.

Zeus slowly turned around. A group of five villagers approached them—two women and three men. He noticed that two of them were carrying pitchforks.

One of the men looked at Zeus with wide eyes. He pointed at Bolt.

"They're Olympians!" he cried.

CHAPTER FIVE

Lost and Found

Zeus held Bolt in front of him.

"Yes, we're Olympians," he said. "Do you have a problem with that?"

"Wow, you sound just like Ares," Hera whispered into his ear.

The man shook his head. "Don't worry. We're not going to turn you in," he said. "We know King Cronus is evil. You Olympians are our only hope!"

Poseidon broke through the web that held him captive and stepped forward. "You know about us?"

A woman with two long braids nodded. "People tell stories of your bravery all over the countryside."

Zeus felt pride surge through him. "We're just doing what we have to do," he said.

"Which is mainly fighting monsters," Poseidon added.

Two of the villagers stepped up to help free Athena and Apollo.

"Would you like to stay with us for a while?" one of the women asked Zeus. "We can keep you safe."

Zeus looked up at the sky. There was still plenty of daylight left.

"Thanks, but we have to keep going," he said. "We have to get to the center of the web as soon as we can."

The man frowned. "We've heard rumors," he

said. "Some say that the spiderwebs are covering up something King Cronus is building in the sky."

"Building in the sky? That doesn't make sense," said Athena.

The man shrugged. "Well, that's what we've heard. Good luck with your journey."

"Word is the Cronies are said to be way west of here," one of the women added. "So you should be safe for a while."

"Thanks," Zeus said. He turned to the other Olympians. "Everybody ready?"

"My clothes are feeling a little bit sticky, but let's move on; I am not picky," replied Apollo.

They marched over the hill and through the village. The villagers waved and clapped as they passed.

"Dude, we're heroes," Poseidon told Zeus. "For real."

"Yeah, maybe we are," Zeus said, grinning.

Then his smile faded. "I'll feel more like a hero when we've rescued the others, though."

Thoughts of Hestia, Demeter, Hades, and Ares kept Zeus quiet for the rest of the day as the Olympians trudged along. He was more eager than ever to reach the center of the web—no matter what waited for them there. But when the sun set, they were still far from their goal.

"Better make camp," Zeus said. They found a sheltered area under some trees—and away from the webs.

Zeus used Bolt to make a fire, and soon they were sitting around the campfire, eating the food that the farmers had given them.

When she finished her meal, Athena took off her aegis. She started to polish it with a scrap of cloth.

"Getting the web off it?" Zeus asked.

"No," she replied. "It's just . . . I remembered

I liked polishing stuff. There was this locket. I'm not sure why I polished it, or even if it was important. But I think it was . . ." Her voice trailed off.

Poseidon leaned into Zeus. "She's more foggy-brained than Pythia," he whispered.

Zeus gave him a warning look. Athena was sitting on the other side of him, and he didn't want her to hear. Sure, she seemed a little . . . confused sometimes. But she was nice. And an Olympian. And Olympians had to stick together.

He glanced over at Athena again. Her gray eyes were wide now. He looked down at the aegis and saw that a face was being revealed as she polished the shield. A horribly scary face, with slithering snakes for hair!

Zeus's eyes widened, too. He started to say something when Athena noticed him looking. She quickly covered the image with the cloth.

"All done," she said.

Zeus was puzzled. *Is she keeping the face secret for a reason?* he wondered. *Or is she just really, really creeped out by it?*

He tried asking her but she moved away. Maybe he was just seeing things because he was tired. Athena was still a mystery. He had a feeling they would learn what the mystery was before too long.

Zeus soon fell asleep, along with the rest of the Olympians. When he woke up at sunrise, he saw Athena leaning over Hera. She was tickling Hera's nose with a feather.

"Wake up, sleepyhead!" she teased.

Zeus braced himself. Hera was not going to like that one bit.

Hera bolted upright, her blue eyes blazing.

"Knock it off!" she howled. Then her eyes grew wide. She grabbed the feather from Athena.

"Athena! You found it! My lost feather!"

CHAPTER SIX
Eye Spy

Zeus couldn't believe it. Hera had lost her peacock feather days ago, and far away. But this one sure looked like her feather—long and green, with a dark blue circle inside a light blue circle inside a dark blue circle. The circles looked kind of like an eye.

The other Olympians were awake now too.

"Hera and her feather are back together," Apollo sang.

"I didn't know it was yours," Athena said. "I found it yesterday when we were walking and tucked it away. Is it a magical object, like the others? What does it do?"

"It can bring us luck," Hera replied.

"We could definitely use some now," Poseidon said, stretching.

Hera stood up. She held the feather in the palm of her hand. "Feather, can you check the paths ahead and find a route that'll get us to the center of the web without getting snared by any more sticky threads?"

The feather floated off her palm and started to slowly float away.

"Hey, come back!" Hera cried. "We're not ready to go yet!"

But the feather kept going. Apollo strummed his lyre. *"Oh, please, Hera's feather, come hither,"* he sang.

Hera turned to him, annoyed. "'Feather, come hither'? That doesn't even rhyme, really. And how is that helping?"

However, it seemed to work. The feather was already winging its way back into her hand. Her eyes got wide.

Apollo smiled.

"I think your feather likes rhymes," he said.

"Don't get any ideas," Hera warned. "This is *my* magical object. Pythia said so."

Apollo held up his hands. "It's all yours."

"I hope your feather does bring us luck," Zeus said. "We need to get to the center of that web."

"It will. Remember how lucky we got when we were looking for Ares's Spear of Fear?" Hera asked. "We found the Amazons who had it right away. And they just handed it over to us!"

Zeus nodded. "You're right. Okay, let's see what your feather can do."

They ate a quick meal and washed up. Then they started back on the path to the center of the web.

"Okay, feather," Hera said. "We need some good luck on this trip."

The feather started to float away again.

"I think it wants us to follow it!" Hera said. "Come on!"

They followed the feather down a new path. The feather slipped easily through the weave of webs, but Zeus still had to whack away with Bolt. Poseidon kept pushing the strands aside with his trident.

"This doesn't seem like a very lucky path," Poseidon grumbled as a sticky strand hit him in the face.

"Well, what do you expect? There are webs everywhere," Hera pointed out. "We can't escape them all."

"Hera, I can't see your feather anymore. It's too far ahead," Zeus told her.

"No problem," she said. "Feather, come hither!" she sang out.

She must've decided she liked Apollo's rhyme after all, thought Zeus.

Almost instantly the feather flew back into Hera's hand. She stopped, staring at it.

"That's weird," she said. "I can see a picture in the eye. It's a tree with webs on it."

Poseidon looked over her shoulder. "I don't see any picture."

"Of course you don't. It's *my* feather," Hera snapped. "I think the feather is showing me what's up ahead."

"Trees and webs. Wow. How did it know that?" Poseidon asked sarcastically.

Hera scowled. "Just wait." They were coming up to a curve in the path.

"Feather, go around that curve," she told it.

The feather didn't move.

"Try rhyming," Apollo suggested.

Hera frowned, but guessed Apollo was on to something. "Okay, feather. Eye spy!"

The feather flew out of her hand and went around the curve.

"Feather, come hither!" Hera called out.

The feather returned to her hand. "Okay, now I see what's next," Hera said, looking into the eye again. "When we go around the curve, we'll find a web with . . . with a square shape in the middle."

They followed the path, and right after the curve they saw a web blocking their way. The shape in its center was a perfect square.

"Big deal!" said Poseidon. "Lots of these webs are like that."

"But not *all* the webs," Hera pointed out.

Zeus sliced through the web with Bolt.

"Maybe we can experiment with your feather later, Hera? For now, let's get moving."

Hera glared at him. "This feather is really going to help us. You'll see."

Luckily, the next stretch of path was clear of webs. As they walked, Athena came up beside Zeus. He could see the bulk of the aegis under her cloak.

She's hiding it, he realized. *Is it because she's scared of that horrid snake-headed face? Or does she just not want anyone else to see it?*

Before he could ask, Athena remarked, "Hera is very proud of her feather."

Zeus nodded. "Well, she waited a long time to find it. Except for Apollo, everybody else already had a magical object. Hades has his helmet that makes him turn invisible. Hestia has a flaming torch that can make fire anywhere. And Demeter has these amazing Magic

Seeds. One seed can bring a whole field alive with crops. And you have the aegis."

Athena looked down at her tunic, and her face got red. "Oh yeah. Well, it's not very special. Hera's feather is cooler."

Now is the time to ask, thought Zeus. "I saw you polishing the shield last night. There was some kind of face on it."

Athena looked surprised. "You must have been seeing things," she told him, and dashed ahead.

What's she hiding? Zeus wondered again. But for now, he decided to let her be.

They marched on. The path led them to an apple orchard, where they had a better view of the open sky. Webs were slung between the trees.

Poseidon ran to the closest tree. He used his trident to pluck one of the apples, pulling it through the web. Then he brushed it on his tunic and took a bite.

"Yum!" he said.

Words quickly appeared on the web in the apple tree: *Enjoy your last meal!*

"Says you!" Poseidon shot back.

"Ignore those stupid messages," Zeus said. "Let's pick as many apples as we can."

They made their way through the orchard. Soon their packs were filled with apples. New messages popped up on the webs every few seconds, though!

Surrender now!

Just give up!

You can't win, losers!

"Well!" huffed Hera. "Just because they are evil, it doesn't mean they have to be rude about it!"

"Like I said, ignore them," said Zeus. "We've got to focus on getting to the center of that web."

He looked up at the sky. A new giant message was popping up, stretched between the clouds.

All fear the Threads of Dread!

Zeus stopped. "The Threads of Dread! That's what Pythia told us to find."

"What's so scary about threads of bread?" Athena asked, reading the writing in the sky. Or trying to, anyway.

"That's Threads of *Dread*," Hera corrected her.

Athena frowned. "That sounds familiar . . . I think."

They kept walking all day, only stopping once to eat lunch and then quickly move on. As the sun set, Zeus stopped and looked around.

They were very close to the center of the web now. The rings of webs were thicker here, and getting tighter and tighter. Strands of the web stretched around them as far as he could see.

We could probably get to the center in an hour or two, he reasoned. *But it would be dark by then. And if there's another monster there . . .*

"We should set up camp," he said reluctantly.

"I see a cave on the left up ahead."

They set up camp just inside the cave. It was long and narrow, and Hera sent the feather to check it out before they all went inside.

"Eye spy!" she commanded. But when the feather came back, all she could see in the eye was darkness.

"Darkness? Really? I could have told you that," said Poseidon. "What else would you expect to see inside a cave?"

"He has a point," Zeus said.

"Zip it, Bolt Breath," Hera warned. "Let's eat."

They sat down to eat a dinner of apples and the last of the cheese the farmers had given them. When they were done, Apollo played his lyre and sang.

"Today Hera found her magical feather.
We are all happy that they're back together.

The feather's powers are yet to be seen,

But Hera is sure they are fit for a queen.

Will it come to our rescue when we're in a pickle?

Well, maybe it won't, but it's good for a tickle."

Hera did not look amused. "Just wait," she said. "This feather will prove to be helpful."

Nobody said anything. They all knew how angry Hera could get if they argued against her. Then a rustling sound outside the cave broke the silence.

"What was that?" Zeus asked, jumping up.

"I'll send out the feather," Hera said. "Feather, eye spy outside the cave!"

The feather floated away but came back when Hera called it. She looked into the eye.

"Spiders!" she yelled. "And one of them is coming this way!"

CHAPTER SEVEN

Turning to Stone

"Calm down," said Poseidon. "We already know there are spiders out there."

Hera shook her head. "These aren't up in the trees. They're crawling and *close*. And one of them is going to be here any second!"

Part of Zeus wondered if Hera might be making up stuff about her feather to make it seem more important.

But better safe than sorry, right? he thought.

"Okay, everybody. Let's go deeper inside the cave," Zeus said. "If there is a spider after us and it doesn't see us, maybe it will go away."

Poseidon rolled his eyes. Still, he didn't argue, and they quickly moved farther into the dark cave. Finally stopping, they pressed their backs against the cold stone wall of the cave.

"Be very quiet," Zeus whispered. "Hera, keep that feather still."

Hera nodded but didn't reply. They all waited, barely daring to breathe.

For a moment everything was perfectly quiet. And then they heard a *skritch, skritch, skritch* sound. Right outside!

That does sound a lot like a spider, Zeus thought.

"Told you!" Hera whispered.

The skittering sound came closer. Zeus couldn't see anything in the darkness of the cave. Then he heard Poseidon yell out.

"Flippin' fangface! A spider just touched my leg!"

Poseidon was so freaked out that he knocked the spider out and raced out of the cave as fast as he could.

"Poseidon!" Zeus cried. "Stop! There could be spiders out there!" He and the others followed, trying to save him from being ensnared. Once outside, the Olympians gasped at what they saw. Dozens of big spiders were lined up at the edge of the woods. Suddenly they came charging at them! Like the spiders they had seen before, each one had a body as big as a melon, and long legs. Dozens of pairs of beady red eyes were fixed on the Olympians.

"Told you!" said Hera.

"That's not very helpful right now," Poseidon pointed out.

Zeus knew they had no choice. They had to fight.

"Bolt, large!" he yelled.

Bolt grew large, and Zeus held it out. "Poseidon, touch your trident!" The Olympians had learned that when they joined their objects, all of the objects became more powerful.

Now Poseidon's trident touched Bolt, and sparks sizzled from the magical weapons.

"I'll add my feather!" Hera said, holding it out. "Athena, your aegis!"

"Um, what?" Athena asked. Her expression was blank, and she made no move to help. Apparently, she didn't understand.

Hera's feather touched Bolt and the trident. A huge blast shot out from the three objects. It struck a heavy tree across the clearing. The tree fell over, landing on a group of spiders as they came out of the woods.

Bam! Boom! The spiders were crushed, their spindly legs sticking out from underneath the tree.

"That was good timing," said Hera. "Told you my feather would bring us good luck."

Another wave of spiders streamed from the woods. They were spitting something at the Olympians—and it didn't look like harmless spider spit!

"Wow, scary AND rude! We're going to need all the luck we can get," quipped Poseidon.

Apollo was picking up rocks. He nodded to Athena. "If we start throwing, we should be able to knock them out."

Bolt, the trident, and the feather were all still glowing with extra power.

Zap! Zeus's thunderbolt hurled a lightning blast at the spiders.

Swooooosh! Water shot from Poseidon's trident and knocked over a bunch of them.

Hera waved her feather. "Feather! Um . . . please be plucky, and make us lucky!" Seconds later two of the spiders charged into each other and knocked each other out.

Bonk! Bonk! Apollo and Athena hurled rocks at the spiders.

Working together, they took down the wave of spiders. Zeus felt like cheering.

"There's more!" Hera yelled. "Look up!"

The huge sky web looked like it was covered by a black blanket. And after a moment, Zeus realized the blanket was moving.

"I think there are a *lot* more," he said, staring. Hundreds and hundreds of spiders streamed toward them from the blanket—which was actually made of spiders!

"Bolt!" Zeus commanded, and a sizzling charge hit the web. It knocked off a few of the spiders, but the rest kept coming.

Then . . . *whoosh!* A thick, sticky strand shot down, aimed right at Hera. She jumped out of the way just in time.

"That was close!" she exclaimed.

Whoosh! Another strand shot down and hit Apollo. He cried out and tried to tear it off, but his hands got stuck in it. The strand wrapped around him, and before anyone could stop it, the strand yanked him up to form a cocoon around him!

"No!" yelled Athena, who was standing next to him. She leaped up and grabbed Apollo's foot, trying to pull him back down.

Suddenly the black wave of spiders on the web parted into two groups, leaving a path open between them.

"What's happening?" Poseidon asked.

"Just keep blasting!" Zeus urged him.

A great shadow fell over everything. Suddenly

a huge spider came crawling down its web on the path toward the Olympians. Its body was as big as a barn. Its red eyes were as huge as wagon wheels. Tiny hairs covered each of its eight long legs.

Zeus blasted the spider with Bolt, but the huge creature didn't even flinch. Poseidon shot a powerful jet of water at it, but the water just streamed off as if Poseidon were giving the spider a shower.

"Athena, watch out!" Zeus warned. The girl was hanging on to Apollo's legs, still trying to get him down. Her feet dangled a foot above the ground.

The enormous spider's eyes had now settled on Athena. Angry, the spider quickly scrambled down the web and over to her. One of its long legs swatted Athena off Apollo.

She landed with a thud on the grass below.

The spider chased her. It loomed over Athena and bared its sharp ivory fangs.

"Nooooooo!" Zeus yelled. He and Poseidon kept blasting the spider with their weapons, but the blasts did no good.

Athena rolled over, trying to get away. The spider pinned her down with a leg. A leg that landed on Athena's cloak, pulling it open.

The aegis shield seemed to gleam. Zeus swore he saw terror in the spider's eyes as it looked at the hideous snake-haired face on the shield.

Then suddenly, the huge spider turned to stone!

CHAPTER EIGHT

The Thread of Cleverness

"S izzling statues!" Poseidon cried. He, Hera, and Zeus stared up at the humongous stone spider in amazement.

The smaller spiders started scrambling around the web, confused. Athena's gray eyes narrowed. She closed her cloak again, hiding the scary-face shield. Then she grabbed the edge of the web and hauled herself up, climbing onto the stone spider statue.

What is she doing? Zeus wondered. Then he saw a shiny chain with a charm dangling from one of the spider's stone fangs. Athena reached out and grabbed the chain. She slipped it around her neck and then jumped down from the web.

"What's that?" Zeus asked, pointing to the charm on the chain.

"It's my locket," Athena said. She opened it and uncurled a long strand of web that was wound inside it.

"It's my magical object," she said proudly. "The Thread of Cleverness!"

"I thought we were looking for the Threads of Dread?" Zeus asked.

"I have a theory about that," Athena said, nodding up at the stone spider. "I'll explain in a minute. First you guys need to all turn around. Apollo, close your eyes!"

"Mmmmfff!" Apollo replied, his mouth still covered in a spiderweb cocoon.

Zeus, Poseidon, and Hera turned around. Behind them Athena opened her cloak.

"Get a good look, spiders!" she yelled. "Come on, look over here!"

The spiders on the web all focused their eyes toward Athena. As soon as they gazed upon the aegis, they turned to stone just like the big spider had. The web dipped low under their new heavier weight.

"All right. We're good," Athena said. She closed the cloak and called to the Olympians. "Let's get Apollo down."

Together they pulled Apollo down from the web and tore the sticky strands of cocoon off him. As he brushed stray pieces from his cloak, Athena told her story.

"The Thread of Cleverness has always

belonged to me," she began. "Its magic lets it twist itself to spell words and send messages."

"So that's how the spiders did it," Hera said, and Athena nodded.

"It can also become as long as it needs to be, and weave itself into whatever I ask," she said. "Oh, and it holds all of my cleverness. When I didn't have it, I was kind of an airhead."

"You can say that again," said Poseidon.

"So how did that enormous spider get it?" Zeus asked.

"The spider's name is Arachne," Athena answered. "She's one of those Creatures of Chaos you talked about. She was trying to take over this village for King Cronus, and I went to stop her. She challenged me to a weaving contest. If I won, she would leave the village alone. I'm an excellent weaver, so I agreed."

"I'm guessing you lost?" Poseidon said.

"Correct," Athena replied. "Before the contest Arachne sent a small spider to steal the locket from me. Without it I didn't have the skills to weave even a place mat. So she won the contest, and then the Cronies came. And then I ended up in that giant urn, and well . . . you know the rest."

Zeus nodded. "So what's your theory about the Thread of Cleverness? Do you think Arachne turned it into the Threads of Dread?"

Athena nodded. "Exactly. With her poison. And then she used the thread's magic to weave this big sky web. Why, I'm still not sure."

Zeus looked up at the web and the stone spiders. "We still need to find Hestia, Demeter, Hades, and Ares. The spiders captured them and stashed them somewhere."

"I think I know what'll help," Athena said. She reached into her pack and took out the instrument that she had made from the reed. This time she kept her fingers away from the top and bottom openings. She held the reed up to her lips and began to blow. A super high note came out. She put her fingers on and off the holes along the reed to play a tune.

As she played, the web began to vibrate and grumble. The stone spiders started to break apart, turning to dust. The pieces of stone started to rain down on the Olympians. It was like stone spider snow! Except it wasn't nice and fluffy like actual snow. In fact, it kinda hurt!

"We should take shelter!" Zeus called out, and everyone ran back into the cave.

Athena kept playing, and the spiders kept crumbling. The web broke apart and turned to dust too. More and more dust fell from the sky.

As the Olympians waited for the dust to clear, they heard four thumps.

Thump! Thump! Thump! Thump!

They all looked at one another. What in Bolt's name could those noises have been? After checking to be sure the coast had cleared of spiders and dust, they ventured outside the cave.

"Hades!" Hera cried, and broke into a run.

The others gasped. There, sprawled on the ground and covered in web dust, were the missing Olympians: Hades, Hestia, Demeter, and Ares!

Zeus reached Hestia first and helped her to her feet. She pulled strands of web from her light brown hair.

"Thirsty," she said, her voice hoarse.

Zeus scanned the scene. Athena was helping Ares, Poseidon had Hades, and Apollo had Demeter.

"Let's get everyone back to the cave," Zeus called out. "I'll start a fire. And, Poseidon, we need water!"

Hestia smiled weakly at Zeus. "I may have spent the last two days trapped in a cocoon, but I can still make fire, thank you very much."

Zeus smiled back. "Of course."

As they gathered by the cave, he felt overwhelmed with happiness. The nine Olympians were together again!

"Is everyone okay?" Zeus asked as Poseidon raised a bubbling spring from the ground.

Hades took a deep drink of water and then wiped his mouth on his sleeve. "Yeah. Being in a cocoon was weird. Kind of like sleeping, only I knew what was happening around me."

Red-haired Demeter nodded. "It wasn't so bad. But I'm glad you saved us."

Ares's red eyes blazed. He waved his spear. "Where are those spiders? Let me at 'em!"

"Too late. Athena turned them all to stone," Hera told him.

Ares looked surprised. "Athena? No way!"

Athena held out her locket. "That big spider, Arachne, stole my cleverness. But it's back here in this locket!"

Hades smiled at her. "In the nick of time. Thanks." He rubbed his belly. "Do you guys have any food? I'm so hungry, I could eat a spider!"

"Ew!" said Hestia, wrinkling her nose. "No way. But I'm pretty hungry too."

Apollo looked into his pack. "I don't think we have much left except for some potatoes."

Athena snapped her fingers. "Oh, I know what would go great with potatoes!"

She took off the aegis and placed it on the ground, carefully covering it with her cloak.

"Aegis, remember that tree I invented?" she asked. "Let's make another olive tree!"

Just like before, a small tree burst from the ground. Athena picked some of the oval, black fruits from its gnarled branches.

"Um, wasn't that invention kind of a failure the first time?" Poseidon asked.

"That's only because I wasn't clever enough then to know what to do with the olives," Athena said. She put them down on a flat rock and started crushing them with another rock. Dark oil pooled around them.

"This oil is great for making fire, and we can pour it on the potatoes after they're cooked," she explained. "It's delicious."

Poseidon stuck his finger into the olive oil and licked it off.

"I have to admit, it's not bad," he said.

"And the olives will taste good too," she said. "Watch." She took the Thread of Cleverness from her locket. "Spell 'pickled,'" she told it.

Instantly the thread formed the word "pickled," and the olives on the tree soon changed. Instead of being hard and shiny, they looked soft and juicy.

"They still have pits," she warned, handing one to everyone. They all began chewing the olives.

"Mmm, this is delicious," said Demeter. "Thank you!"

"I'll get the potatoes onto the fire," Apollo offered.

Soon they were all munching on fried potatoes with crushed, pickled olives. Hestia, Demeter, Hades, and Ares were full of questions about what the others had been up to.

"I've already written a song about it," said Apollo. Then he picked up his lyre and began to sing.

"Four were captured and five were spared.
The remaining five were very scared.
But on they went, to save the four,

Knowing that dangers were in store.

In sticky webs they all got stuck,

But Hera's feather brought them luck.

Then the spider army found the five.

It did not look like they'd survive.

Until Athena found her thread,

And every spider wound up dead!"

Everyone laughed and clapped. Their bellies were full and the fire was dying, so they went inside the cave to sleep. In the morning Zeus was up first as usual. He went outside to greet the sunrise.

Then he froze. In the daylight the damage Athena had done to the web was obvious. Most of it had been torn down. Now he could see what the web had been hiding.

Somebody was building an enormous temple high in the clouds!

CHAPTER NINE

Follow the Leader

G uys! You've gotta see this!" Zeus called, and the other Olympians swiftly joined him.

"Is that . . . a temple?" Hades asked, unbelieving.

"It sure looks like it," Poseidon said. "A temple in the clouds."

They all gazed at the amazing sight for a moment. Impossibly, the huge marble temple sat on top of fluffy white clouds without falling.

It was bigger than any temple on earth, with a domed roof and columns taller than the tallest trees. Long strands of web still hung from the clouds around it. Now they sagged low, some of them almost touching the ground.

"We met some people who told us a rumor," Zeus said. "A rumor that Cronus was using the giant webs to hide something he was building in the sky. I guess this is it."

"Why does he need a temple in the sky?" Hestia wondered.

"Because he thinks he's better than everybody else," Poseidon replied. "He wants to look down on all of us."

"Pythia told us that we would have to face Cronus soon," Zeus reminded everyone. "I guess now is the time."

Everyone was quiet for a second. Ares spoke up first.

"Let's fight him! We'll take him down!" he yelled.

"Calm down. I mean, are we really ready?" Hestia said. "Half of us just got captured by spiders. We're weak. How are we supposed to fight King Cronus and his army of Cronies?"

"With our weapons!" Ares cried, shaking his spear.

"We've still got half a day's walk before we stand below the temple," Zeus said. "Let's get moving."

The trip to the temple was made easier by the strands of the web. As they each grabbed a strand and began to climb, many of the Olympians were curious to learn more about Athena. As they huffed and puffed their way upward, they spoke every now and then.

"I still can't believe you're smart now," Poseidon said bluntly.

Athena shrugged. "Yeah, I guess I was acting pretty silly before."

"So, just how smart are you now?" Hades asked. "Like, do you know the square root of 86,754?"

"Hey, that's my lucky number!" Poseidon quipped, grinning.

Athena thought briefly. "It's 294.5403198 . . . There are more digits. How far do you want me to go?"

"That's awesome!" said Hades.

"I've got one for you! What's faster? A falcon or a golden eagle?" Apollo asked Athena.

"Well, if you're talking about a peregrine falcon, it would beat a golden eagle when they're both diving for prey," Athena replied.

Hestia clapped her hands. "This is fun! Athena, how much lava can a volcano hold?"

"Well, it depends on the size of a volcano,"

Athena replied. "But volcanoes don't actually hold lava. The hot liquid rock beneath the surface is called magma. It's not called lava until the volcano spews it out."

"Cool!" said Poseidon. "Zeus, come on. Ask her something."

"Thanks, anyway," Zeus said, quickly climbing ahead.

He knew he should have been happy that Athena had recovered her cleverness. But he couldn't help feeling a little jealous.

I'm supposed to be the leader of the Olympians, he thought. *Pythia said so. I might not have liked the idea at first, but I'm getting used to it. So, what happens if everybody decides that Athena is a better leader than I am? Just because she's smarter?*

Zeus tried to shake off the thought. He had much bigger things to worry about. *Really* big things. Like King Cronus and his Cronies.

As Zeus had guessed, it took the Olympians about half a day to get close to the temple in the clouds. Now that they were near, the temple seemed even bigger. Strands of web hung down it, some of them still touching the ground.

Hera looked at Zeus.

"Okay, Boltbrain," she said. "What now?"

Everyone was looking at him. His brothers and sisters: Hera, Hestia, Demeter, Hades, and Poseidon. His friends: Apollo, Ares, and now Athena. They expected *him* to decide what they should do.

I am *a leader*, Zeus realized. *Now I've got to act like one.*

He looked up at the temple. The thick, fluffy clouds surrounding it made it hard to see what was going on up there.

"We climb," Zeus said. "But for all we know, there could be an army of Cronies waiting for us when we get to the top. So we need a plan."

"I could put on my helmet and scout it out up there before we all go," Hades suggested.

Zeus shook his head. "No. I'm not losing anybody again. We stick together."

"Well, then, I'll send my feather," Hera said.

Zeus nodded. "Good idea," he said, and Hera sent her feather to spy on the temple in the clouds. When it came back to her, she looked into its eye.

"You were right, Zeus!" she said. "There's an army of Cronies up there. They're lined up in rows. In battle formation!"

Zeus frowned. "Then we've got to hit them hard right from the start. Let's take stock of our weapons."

"I've got my torch," offered Hestia.

Demeter clutched the pouch of seeds that dangled from her belt. "I've got my seeds, but I'd hate to have to use them in battle. It's much nicer when they can grow crops for people.

Ares jumped in front of her. "The Cronies will give up when they see my Spear of Fear!"

"The Cronies are way bigger than your spear," Hera pointed out. She held up her feather. My Feather of Eyes can bring us luck."

"We're gonna need it," said Poseidon. "Even though Bolt and my trident are a pretty powerful combo."

Apollo shrugged. "I've got a pouch full of stone spider rocks. That's something."

"And I've got my aegis, which invents things," Athena said. "And my Thread of Cleverness."

An idea popped into Zeus's mind. "Athena, how strong is that thread?"

"It's pretty much unbreakable," she replied. "Legend says that only a magic blade can cut through it. And I've never heard of anyone having such a blade."

Zeus grinned. "Then I think I've got an idea. Athena and Apollo, it involves you."

Zeus told the Olympians his plan. They put it into action, first finding sturdy long web strands hanging down from the clouds right next to one another.

"Okay, Athena, Ares, Hestia, Demeter, and Hera, you'll line up on the left. Apollo, Poseidon, Hades, and I will line up on the right. You know what to do."

"First, a circle," Hera suggested. The nine Olympians formed a circle and each put a hand into the center.

"Gooooooo, Olympians!" they cheered, raising their arms into the air.

Then Athena and Apollo each grabbed on to a web strand and began the climb to the clouds. The others followed, one at a time. Just before they reached the top, Athena and Apollo stopped. Athena took the Thread of Cleverness from her locket and held one end. Then she gave the other end to Apollo.

"All right, everyone," Zeus called out softly. "Let's do this!"

Athena and Apollo climbed on top of the cloud. Still holding the ends of the Thread of Cleverness, Athena ran to the left and Apollo ran to the right. The rest of the Olympians climbed up behind them.

Rows and rows of huge Cronies were waiting for them on top of the clouds, not more than a hundred yards away.

Each half-giant Crony was as tall as a willow tree. Polished iron helmets protected their heads, and each one held a long spear in his massive fist. With a thunderous battle cry they charged at the line of Olympians facing them.

"All right, Olympians. Charge!" Zeus yelled.

On his command, Ares, Hestia, Demeter, and Hera ran left to join Athena. Zeus, Poseidon, and Hades ran behind Apollo.

Before the first line of Cronies could change direction and follow, they ran right into the Thread of Cleverness. Stretched out between Athena and Apollo, it was nearly invisible.

"Whoooooaaaaaaa!"

The first line of Crony soldiers tripped over the thread and tumbled right off the clouds!

"Yes!" Zeus cheered.

The second line of Cronies was right behind them. They tripped too, and dozens more Cronies went tumbling off the clouds.

"This is too easy!" Poseidon told Zeus.

Then the third line of soldiers charged. By now they had begun to realize something was wrong. A few of them tumbled over the thread. Others tried to quickly stop, and they bumped

into one another. One big Crony bumped right into Apollo, knocking him down.

"Noooooo!" Apollo cried as the Thread of Cleverness slid from his fingers. The thread instantly coiled back into Athena's hand.

Zeus had known the thread wouldn't take out all of the Cronies, but it had been a good start.

"Next wave!" Zeus yelled.

Hestia jumped in front of Athena, and Poseidon jumped in front of Apollo. Hestia aimed her torch at the feet of the approaching Cronies. Fire sprang up where she pointed.

"Ow! Ow! Ow!" they screamed, jumping up and down. More of them leaped off the cloud to get away.

Swoooooooosh! Poseidon shot a blast of water from his trident, knocking a bunch more off.

"Okay. Now, everyone!" Zeus commanded.

Ares shot his Spear of Fear at the Cronies.

The spear zipped through the line of attackers, knocking the spears out of their hands. Hades put on his helmet and ran around the Cronies, kicking them hard in the shins.

"Ow! Ow! Ow! Quit it!" they yelled. But when they looked down, they couldn't see anyone attacking them.

Thunk! Thunk! Thunk! Hera and Demeter hurled rocks Apollo had given them as hard as they could, aiming for the Cronies' knees.

Zap! Zap! Zap! Zeus hurled lightning bolt blasts at the Cronies, knocking them down one by one.

The wave of Cronies was thinning fast.

We're winning! Zeus thought in excitement. It was time for one big move. . . .

"Olympians, together!" he called out, holding Bolt above his head.

The other Olympians ran to him, holding

up their magical objects too. Once they combined, their power would be enough to knock out the rest of the Cronies. At least Zeus hoped it would.

Just as the objects were about to touch, a dark shadow fell across them. The Olympians looked up.

A giant man twice as tall as the Cronies loomed over the Olympians. A gold crown sat on top of his bushy black hair. He grinned, revealing a smile with a missing front tooth. The Olympians had knocked that tooth out a while back.

"Well, if it isn't the Olympians," he bellowed, laughing. "I was hoping you'd show up."

"King Cronus!" Zeus cried.

CHAPTER TEN

King Cronus

The evil king picked Zeus up with one hand, then held him close in front of his face.

"Welcome Zeus, the fearless leader of the Olympians," he said in a mocking voice.

"Bolt!" Zeus yelled, and his magical weapon zapped Cronus with electric energy. The Titan flinched but didn't lose his grip. With his free hand, he grabbed the lightning bolt from Zeus and tossed it away.

 102

"Enough of this child's play," Cronus said. "I need to have a word with you."

Zeus's legs dangled from Cronus's hand as the king stomped toward the temple. Zeus looked down and saw the other Olympians were still fighting off the remaining Cronies below. He hoped they'd be okay.

Cronus stopped in front of the temple and waved his free hand toward it.

"Welcome to my kingdom!" he said, in a booming voice. "I call it Mount Titan, and it shall be a home for immortals—Titan immortals."

Zeus had met many of the Titans. Most of them had been horrible, nasty, and cruel.

"So why are you telling me?" he asked in the bravest voice he could manage.

"Because unlike your other puny companions, you've got something special," Cronus said. "So leave them behind. Stay here on Mount Titan. We can rule together!"

Zeus's mind was spinning. Why would Cronus want an Olympian, his enemy, to rule with him? It must be some kind of trick.

Play along, he told himself. *See what you can find out.*

"That's an interesting idea," Zeus said. "It's pretty cool up here. I like it."

"Pretty cool? It's magnificent! The finest kingdom ever created!" Cronus boomed.

"Sure, of course it is," Zeus said quickly. "So, what happens if I join you? What happens to the other Olympians? And the mortals down there on Earth?"

"They shall live to serve us!" Cronus declared. "We shall enslave each and every one. Nothing shall stop us!" Then he let out an evil laugh. "Ha-ha! Ha-ha!"

Zeus nodded. "Well, in that case . . ." He held out a hand. "Bolt! Return!"

Bolt instantly returned to Zeus's hand. Using Bolt like a sword, he brought it down hard on Cronus's huge wrist. Crying out in pain, Cronus opened his hand, and Zeus tumbled out. Quickly he tucked Bolt back into his belt and grabbed on to the side of the temple, stopping his fall. Then he pulled himself up onto the roof.

"Foolish boy!" Cronus thundered, his black eyes flashing. He swatted at Zeus, but Zeus whipped Bolt out again and zapped the Titan's hand. With a growl of rage Cronus made a fist and moved to smash him. But Zeus darted out of the way just in time.

Boom! Cronus's fist slammed down. The temple roof shook wildly, and Zeus could see the marble cracking beneath his feet. He tried

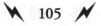

to scramble down from the roof, but Cronus grabbed him by the collar.

"How dare you reject my offer?" he asked, holding Zeus up in the air again. "That was your one chance. Now I shall destroy you, just as I shall destroy all the other Olympians!"

"Why did you think I would ever want to join the Titans anyway?" Zeus asked as he struggled to get out of Cronus's grasp. "You guys are all huge jerks!"

A wicked grin spread across the Titan's face. "Maybe because you are my son!" Cronus announced.

The words hit Zeus like a ton of bricks. They took his breath away. "That's a lie!" he screamed.

Suddenly he felt something wrap around his waist. The Thread of Cleverness! He saw Cronus's eyes grow wide. Then that thread yanked him right out of the Titan king's grasp!

Zeus's stomach flipped as he felt himself falling . . . and falling. Then . . . *Thud*! He landed on a thick, fluffy cloud. Jumping to his feet, he saw Athena standing right next to him, holding the Thread of Cleverness. "Thanks!" he told her. But inside he was still shaken by what Cronus said. Was it true?

"We've got to get out of here," she replied. "Let's go!"

Zeus nodded. They ran, quickly catching up to the other Olympians. Some of them had already started climbing down a strand of spiderweb. Zeus couldn't help noticing that the clouds were now littered with fallen Cronies.

"Nice job, everyone," he said.

Hera grinned. "We worked together," she explained. "But I don't think we can take down Cronus, even working together. Let's go. Hurry!"

The clouds shook as Cronus angrily stomped

toward the Olympians. Athena started down the dangling web strands, with Zeus right behind her. Weakened from the battle, the web that remained began to crumble under them.

"Quick! Touch objects!" Zeus yelled. "We can make an energy bubble!"

The others quickly scrambled to stand together on the now flimsy web, holding out their objects.

"Oh no!" Demeter yelled. "Poseidon, you just poked a hole in my bag with your trident!"

"Never mind. Put the objects all together," Zeus urged. Once they did, he cried out, "Massive energy bubble!"

White light shot out from the touching magical weapons. It formed a bubble, surrounding them as the last strand of web broke away. Instead of crashing to the ground, the nine Olympians floated safely inside the bubble. Once on the ground, it popped.

"Will Cronus come after us?" Hera wondered, staring up worriedly.

"I'm not sure," Zeus said. "He might have a hard time getting down from the clouds with the web gone. But let's run, just in case."

Hearts pounding, they raced away from the temple in the clouds. The land around them looked different from how it had before. Rows and rows of olive trees were growing all around them.

Athena was amazed. "How did this happen?" she asked as they ran.

"One of my magic seeds must have fallen out and somehow mixed with your olives to plant trees," Demeter said, clutching her damaged bag.

Athena nodded. "Wow, impressive!"

"Indeed it is!" The voice came from a foggy mist in front of them. The Olympians slowed to a stop. They had all seen that mist before.

The figure of a dark-haired woman appeared in the mist.

"Pythia!" Apollo cried.

The oracle smiled at them. She took off her glasses and rubbed the mist's steam from them with the edge of her cloak.

"Ah, there you are," she said. "All nine of you. Excellent! You have done well."

"I'm not so sure about that," Zeus said. "We were supposed to defeat Cronus, and we failed!"

"I said you would face Cronus soon, and you did," Pythia said. "Bravely. And now Athena has her Thread of Cleverness. Hera is reunited with her Feather of Eyes."

"I can use it to spy on things," Hera said, and Pythia nodded.

"Yes, that is one of its helpful powers," she said.

"So, what's next?" Zeus asked.

111

Pythia closed her eyes. "I see that this place will become a great city . . . a city full of liver trees."

"Do you mean olive trees?" Athena asked.

Pythia opened her eyes. "Right. Olives. Sorry, the mist somehow fogs my glasses. Anyway, the people of this city will learn how to use the olives. They will honor you by naming the city Athens."

Athena beamed. "Cool!"

Pythia closed her eyes again. "I also see King Cronus gathering the Titans together in the future. There will be a battle. But not just yet. You are not ready to defeat them. You will need help still from other Olympians."

Pythia looked at Apollo. "Before the battle, you must find your twin sister, Artemis."

Apollo laughed with glee. "*I hope we find my sister, for I have surely missed her,*" he sang.

Pythia nodded. "She is being held by the

Titan Crius on an island far away. You must get there and rescue her before continuing on your quest."

"But where exactly is she?" Zeus asked.

Pythia squinted. "She is in the land of triplets. Wait. Sorry. These things are fogging up again!" Pythia wiped her glasses. "Ah, that's better. She is in Tripoli. Go there and find her—and she will help you battle Cronus and his army."

As usual, when she finished speaking, Pythia started to slowly disappear into the mist. As she faded away, Zeus remembered she hadn't let them know of a new magical object to seek. But it was too late now.

"Well, looks like we've got some more walking to do," Poseidon sighed. "What a surprise!"

"We should pick some olives to take with us," Athena suggested.

They filled their packs with olives before

they headed down the road. As they walked, Apollo started to write a song about the battle in the clouds. And Ares was swinging his spear around, bragging about how many Cronies he had taken down.

Meanwhile, Zeus was deep in thought.

Was Cronus really his father? He didn't want to believe it, but deep down he feared it might be true. That would explain why his mother, Rhea, couldn't be with him and his brothers and sisters.

Cronus is an evil jerk, he thought. *I hate the idea of him and the Titans ruling everyone from the sky. The Olympians should take over that cloud temple!*

Suddenly Hera stopped in her tracks, staring hard at her feather.

"Um, bad news, guys. We have company already. A Crony army is behind us!"

They had been followed! Like on all of their quests, it looked like they would have to either hide or fight another battle before rescuing their next Olympian.

We will find the other Olympians, Zeus vowed as the Olympians picked up their pace to widen their lead. *And together, one day we will storm Mount Titan. We will claim it for ourselves. And we'll call it . . . Mount Olympus!*